GW00854815

MARY-ANN'S GRANDMA'S GHOST STORY

Muriel A. Kingsley

ARTHUR H. STOCKWELL LTD
Torrs Park Ilfracombe Devon
Established 1898
www.ahstockwell.co.uk

By the same author:
Two Little Mice and Mary-Ann

ISBN 978-0-7223-3981-7
Printed in Great Britain by
Arthur H. Stockwell Ltd
Torrs Park   Ilfracombe
Devon

Mary-Ann's Grandma's Ghost Story

It was twilight and soon it would be Mary-Ann's bedtime. As usual Mary-Ann skipped down the grassy hill, following the dusty path to her grandma's adorable, magical house, to listen to one of her many thrilling bedtime stories.

Her little black and white cat, Tibs, was always nearby, chasing a butterfly or trying to catch her own tail.

Sometimes Mary-Ann would sleep over with the other grandchildren in Grandma's heavenly high bed.

Grandma's adorable,
        magical house.

Sometimes her father would join them to enjoy the sweet calmness of his mother's voice.

"Mary-Ann, my precious, come and sit next to me," said her charming grandma, as she leant back cheerfully in her old mahogany rocking chair, while the two older grandchildren and the youngest of her four sons sat quietly around her.

It was a dark, moonless night, with not a single star shining in the sky. A small kerosene lamp shone in one corner of the room, and the flickering shadows danced to the music of the night.

Grandma pulled her brightly coloured shawl loosely around her shoulders, then sat with her hands folded on her lap.

As usual she began one of her many thrilling tales:

Long ago when I was a wee girl . . .

She paused for a moment, then she reached out and picked up a large white enamel mug, full of home-made drinking chocolate mixed with cane sugar, nutmeg and fresh coconut milk. She sipped slowly, looking around the poorly lit room; then she took another sip of hot chocolate from the mug.

"Ah, this is good," she said, with a smile on her sweet face.

Grandma sat with her hands folded
on her lap.

She removed her half-moon spectacles from her face, carefully folded them and placed them on top of the Bible which was sitting on the bureau. The Bible was the only book in Mary-Ann's grandma's house.

After a pause she began again:

Tonight I shall tell you about the man who lived at No. 13 Logwood Lane. He would come out at night, when most people were in their beds. He would knock on their doors and then disappear into the dark, mysterious night, leaving them shaking with fear and anger.

She paused for another long moment, then started again after clearing her throat:

The man who lived at
No. 13 Logwood Lane.

The horrid man demanded that his mother should stay up until he got home, no matter how late it was; and if she fell asleep, he would undoubtedly shout at her: "Where is my dinner? Where is my dinner? Get me my dinner now!"

She would scream for help, but no one came to her rescue because everyone was afraid of that pig of a son.

The abuse went on for many long years until, one ghastly night, just as he started to scream at his mother, he fell down dead!

"Heart attack," the doctor gravely reported.

Two days later he was buried in the ancient graveyard with only the mother and a few of her friends attending.

After the quiet burial, the mother went home, hoping that now her son was dead she might be able to live a peaceful life and forget the awful things that he had done to her. But it was not to be. At night she could feel his presence; she could smell his musky cigar; and as soon as she drifted off into sleep he appeared at the end of her bed, with his terrible temper and his annoying, booming voice.

"Where's my dinner? Where's my dinner? Get me my dinner."

She sat up suddenly in her bed.

She cried out, "Oh, Lord!" and she sat up suddenly in her bed. She looked around the dark room. "Was that a dream?" she asked herself. Then she cried out again, "Oh, my Lord, my son has come back from the grave to torment me!"

The nightmare continued – night after night of endless torment. Then, one drizzling Sunday morning after she had eaten her meagre breakfast, she packed a small bag with her few belongings and left. She said a tearful goodbye to her neighbours, and then walked away, never to return. She could not live with that ghost any longer.

However, he still lingers on at No. 13 Logwood Lane. To this day he is still known to knock on people's doors and then disappear into the dark, mysterious night.

Mary-Ann's grandma reached out and took the enamel mug. She drank the last drop of chocolate, which was quite cold by then. She dabbed her lips with her red and white polka-dot handkerchief. She had come to the end of her ghost story.

"That's it for tonight," she said.

He still lingers on
   at No. 13 Logwood Lane.

Then suddenly the lightning flashed and the semi-dark room was flooded with light. At almost the same moment there was an almighty clap of thunder. The rain pounded furiously down on the zinc roof of the house. The wind wrestled with the windowpane. An old cat-faced owl hooted from a nearby tree. The frogs and toads gargled as they leapt for shelter.

An old cat-faced owl.

Mary-Ann, and the other very frightened grandchildren, took shelter underneath their grandma's awfully dark bed.

The light went out. The house was in complete darkness. It was very scary.

Mary-Ann could hear her grandma groping in her apron pockets to find a box of matches. She relit the lamps.

"Hooray!" they all shouted as the room came back to life again.

Then there came a loud knock on the door – an anxious knock.

"Who on earth could that be in this rain and at this time of night?" said Mary-Ann's grandma.

Everyone's hair stood on end – except for Grandma's, who was as fearless as the goddess of courage. Mary-Ann and the other children were shaking with fright.

"Maybe it's Mr Whatshisname. You know – the man from No. 13," Mary-Ann stammered from underneath her grandma's very dark bed.

"Stop it!" Mary-Ann's uncle replied. "The man has been dead for many years, so he can't knock on the door – anyway, I don't believe in ghosts." His voice was trembling.

There came another knock on the door, louder this time.

Tibs popped her little shiny head out from under the end of Grandma's patchwork bedspread to get a glimpse of what was going on.

Mary-Ann's grandma slowly got up from the old rocking chair; she pulled her shawl tightly around her shoulders to protect herself from the chill of the night. Her long flowing skirt danced gracefully around her ankles as she calmly glided across the poorly lit room to the front door.

As she gently opened the door, they all held their breath, wrapping themselves more tightly in their blankets and huddling more closely together.

"Ah, it's you. Come in," she said, as she beckoned Mary-Ann's father into the half-lit room.

Tibs popped her shiny head out.

Everyone breathed a huge sigh of relief. Mary-Ann crept out quickly from her hiding place.

"I never want to listen to another ghost story as long as I live," she mumbled. She rushed over to her father, who was still standing in the middle of the room. "Papa," she whispered as she reached out and took hold of his hand.

He knew she was ready to go home. He put an old worn-out hat on Mary-Ann's head and wrapped an old blanket around her to guard her from the drizzling rain.

"Tibs, where are you? Come on – it's time to go home," said Mary-Ann.

She lovingly picked up her beautiful black and white cat in her little arms.

"Hold on tight!" said Mary-Ann's father as he scooped them both up in his strong arms.

They bade the others goodnight: "Goodnight, Grandma; goodnight, everyone. I'll see you tomorrow," said Mary-Ann.

They went up the wet, soggy hill, through the dark, moonless, starless night, with the rain drizzling down on their faces.

They finally got home just as it stopped raining. Mary-Ann's father took her to her warm bed.

"Goodnight, Mary-Ann. Sweet dreams," he whispered.

"Goodnight, Papa. Sleep good," she said.

"Goodnight, Mary-Ann.
Sweet dreams."